What's the time, Mr Wolf?

Colin Hawkins

What's the time, Mr Wolf?

What's the time, Mr Wolf?

What's the time, Mr Wolf?

What's the time, Mr Wolf?

What's the time, Mr Wolf?

What's the time, Mr Wolf?

What's the time, Mr Wolf?

What's the time, Mr Wolf?

What's the time, Mr Wolf?

What's the time, Mr Wolf?

What's the time, Mr Wolf?

6 o'clock, time for bed.

First published in Great Britain 1983
by William Heinemann Ltd
Published 1994 by Mammoth
an imprint of Reed Consumer Books Ltd
Michelin House, 81 Fulham Road, London SW3 6RB
and Auckland, Melbourne, Singapore and Toronto
Reprinted 1995, 1996, 1997, 1998

ISBN 0 7497 1747 5

A CIP catalogue record for this title is available from the British Library

Printed in Hong Kong